S0-CFZ-057

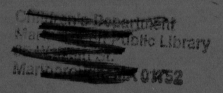
Children's Department
Ma... Public Library
...
Marlboro... ... 01752

Ingram
5/63
12.00

I'LL DO THE RIGHT THING

JEAN ALICIA ELSTER

ILLUSTRATED BY
NICOLE TADGELL

MARLBOROUGH PUBLIC LIBRARY
CHILDREN'S ROOM
MARLBORO, MASS. 01752

JUDSON PRESS ■ VALLEY FORGE

To my sister and friend,
Norma Gwynn Fuqua,
and my nephew, Jimmy   —JAE

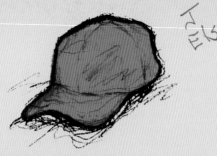

For Reverend and Mrs. H. Allen
Tadgell, with love, —NST

I'LL DO THE RIGHT THING

©2003 by Judson Press, Valley Forge, PA 19482. All rights reserved.

No part of this publication may be reproduced, stored in a retrieval system, or transmitted in any form or by any means, electronic, mechanical, photocopying, recording, or otherwise, without the prior permission of the copyright owner, except for brief quotations included in a review of the book.

Joe Joe's library book, *Ralph Bunche: The Life of a Peacemaker*, is a fictional creation. The information attributed to that book was gleaned from the following sources: Ralph J. Bunche, *Ralph J. Bunche: Selected Speeches and Writings*, Charles P. Henry, ed. (Ann Arbor: The University of Michigan Press, 1995). Jim Haskins, *Ralph Bunche: A Most Reluctant Hero* (New York: Hawthorn Books, Inc., 1974). Peggy Mann, *Ralph Bunche: UN Peacemaker* (New York: Coward, McCann & Geoghegan, Inc., 1975). Brian Urquhart, *Ralph Bunche: An American Life* (New York: W. W. Norton & Company, 1993).

Vintage photography provided by AP/Wide World Photos (pages 21, 29) and Bettman/Corbis (page 23). The Scripture verse on page 3 is quoted from *The Holy Bible*, King James Version.

Library of Congress Cataloging-in-Publication Data

Elster, Jean Alicia.
      I'll Do the Right Thing / Jean Alicia Elster ; illustrated by Nicole Tadgell.
p. cm. – (Joe Joe in the city)

SUMMARY: When Joe Joe's friend Tyrone wants him to join his gang at school, Joe Joe finds that listening to his grandmother and learning about the statesman Ralph J. Bunche help him decide what to do.
ISBN 0-8170-1408-X (alk. paper)
      [1. Gangs—Fiction. 2. Conduct of life—Fiction. 3. Grandmothers—Fiction. 4. African Americans—Fiction. 5. Bunche, Ralph J. (Ralph Johnson), 1904-1971—Fiction.] I. Tadgell, Nicole, 1969- ill. II. Title. III. Series.

PZ7 .E529 Ij 2003
[Fic]—dc21   2002276242
Printed in China
09 08 07 06 05 04 03 02
10 9 8 7 6 5 4 3 2 1

Blessed are the peacemakers: for they
shall be called the children of God.

Matthew 5:9

Joe Joe was sitting at one of the computers at the Bethune Branch Public Library. He had been staring at the screen for a while now. He only wanted to look busy. He had run into the library right after school because he didn't want his friends to catch up with him. He didn't care so much if Kalia saw him. But he definitely did not want to talk to Tyrone.

Mrs. Morgan, the librarian, came up behind him and whispered, "Joe Joe Rawlings, don't you think it's about time you actually looked up a book?" Even though he could barely hear her, Joe Joe jumped in his seat when she spoke.

"Ma'am?" Joe Joe turned around and looked up.

"Enter the name Ralph J. Bunche. Bunche is spelled with an 'e' at the end."

Joe Joe entered the name on the keyboard. A long list of books filled the screen.

"Select the first title, Joe Joe," Mrs. Morgan instructed him. When he did so, she pointed to a row of numbers that appeared on the screen.

"That's the call number. Write it down; it tells us where to find the book on the shelves."

Joe Joe jotted down the number and then followed Mrs. Morgan as she walked to the back of the library.

"*Ralph Bunche: The Life of a Peacemaker*," Mrs. Morgan read the title out loud as she pulled the book from the shelf. Then she handed it to Joe Joe.

"He was an American," Mrs. Morgan explained. "An African American. But he worked to help other countries solve their problems when they couldn't do it themselves."

Joe Joe just looked at her with a puzzled look on his face.

"He was a peacemaker. You'll understand what I mean after you read the book," she assured him with a smile.

"OK, Mrs. Morgan. Thanks." Joe Joe gathered up his book bag and checked out the book before heading for the door.

Kalia was walking by the library as Joe Joe pushed opened the door. She saw him and called out, "Tyrone's been looking for you."

Joe Joe joined her as they both headed for home.

"I told him you were probably in the library, but he didn't believe me!" she said with a smirk. They walked a block or so without talking. Then Kalia asked, "What do you think about the trouble at school?"

"I dunno..." Joe Joe shrugged. He had seen Tyrone talking with a group of kids during recess, but he didn't know what they had been whispering about. He *did* have the feeling that it was going to be trouble, just by the way the other kids had been looking at Tyrone.

Before he could say any more, Kalia continued, "Tyrone says he's gonna do something about it.... Do you think he can?"

"Maybe...." Joe Joe looked at her expectantly, hoping she would tell him more about what was going on.

"Well, here's my street. See you tomorrow, Joe Joe!" Kalia waved and turned the corner.

Joe Joe walked the rest of the way home alone. He was thinking about Tyrone again and what kind of trouble might be brewing at school.

As he walked into the house, he called out, "Hi, Grandma!"

Grandma looked up from the counter and smiled as Joe Joe dropped his book bag and his library book in the kitchen and headed straight to the bathroom to wash his hands. He was hungry and wanted some of the sugar cookies he could smell in the air. His grandma made the *best* sugar cookies in the world.

He sat down at the kitchen table and asked her, "Did Mama and Dad leave for work yet?"

"Um-hum," Grandma answered, placing a plate of still-warm cookies in front of him. "Just a few minutes ago."

Joe Joe's mouth fell open as he looked at the cookies. "What happened to them, Grandma? They look different!"

"The cookies?" His grandmother laughed. "It's the same recipe, Joe Joe. I just sprinkled a little cinnamon on them. They're still good. Here, try one!"

Hesitantly, Joe Joe took a bite, chewed slowly, and then smiled.

"Yeah, they're still good, Grandma!"

"Still good, Gramma!" a small voice echoed from under the table.

Joe Joe grinned and peeked under the tablecloth. "Hi, Brandon!" Joe Joe's little brother was under the table playing with his truck. Brandon stuck his head out and giggled. Grandma popped a piece of cookie in his open mouth.

"Oh, Joe Joe...."

He could tell by his grandmother's tone of voice that he might not like what he was about to hear.

"Your mom and dad got a letter from school, today..." she continued as she picked up an envelope that was on the table and pulled out the paper inside.

Joe Joe's heart started to race. He didn't remember getting into any trouble at school lately, but....

"It was sent to all the parents. Looks like there's a gang problem at your school. Can you believe it?" Grandma shook her head in disbelief. "A gang problem in elementary school...."

Joe Joe shifted in his seat. So maybe *that* was the trouble Tyrone was getting involved with!

"Your parents want to talk to you about what's going on, but it'll have to wait until tomorrow morning when they're both home...."

Before she could finish her sentence, there was a knock on the back door. Tyrone was standing at the screen door.

"Hey, Joe Joe, can you come out?" Tyrone called into the kitchen.

Joe Joe looked at his grandmother.

"Sure," she answered for him.

Joe Joe slowly walked out the back door. He knew what Tyrone had on his mind. They walked over to the middle of the small backyard.

"Has anyone from KC's gang talked to you, yet?"

"No. Why?" Joe Joe asked.

"What about the Old Men?" Tyrone demanded.

"No—what's going on, Tyrone? I've never even *heard* of the Old Men!"

"Listen," Tyrone leaned forward and lowered his voice. "They're another gang—older guys from the high school. They're moving in on KC's gang and trying to recruit younger kids now."

"At *our* school?"

"Yeah, man! You mean no one's talked to you yet?"

Joe Joe shook his head.

"Well, watch out. Sometimes, they use bullies...."

"Bullies? Why?"

"They try to rough you up—scare you into joining up with them. That's what I wanted to talk to you about. I'm not afraid of any of them. I'm putting together my own crew. Why don't you join up with me and my boys? We can watch each other's backs and beat any of the other gangs."

Just then, Tyrone looked over at the screen door and saw Joe Joe's grandmother standing at the door. Joe Joe swallowed hard when he saw her too.

"Listen, I'll talk to you later," Tyrone said to Joe Joe. "Goodbye, ma'am," he called to Joe Joe's grandmother. She waved from where she stood at the door.

Joe Joe wasn't sure how much she had overheard.

"Joe Joe, come inside. I want to show you something." Grandma held the door open for him. "Have you seen this before?"

Joe Joe looked at the framed picture hanging on the kitchen wall—at least, he'd always thought it was a picture. But now he could tell it was words embroidered on cloth.

"Blessed are the peacemakers," Joe Joe read. "What does *peacemaker* mean, Grandma?"

She smiled and kissed him on the forehead. "Think about it while you do your homework. Then we'll talk."

Upstairs in his room, Joe Joe looked at the title of his book as he lay across his bed—*Ralph Bunche: The Life of a Peacemaker*. There was that word again—*peacemaker*.

When Ralph Johnson Bunche was born in Detroit in 1903, no one would have guessed what he would achieve during his lifetime. Ralph Bunche was the first African American to receive a doctorate—the highest degree that can be earned from a college or university—in political science. He was the first African American to be awarded the Nobel Peace Prize. In addition, when he retired, he was the highest ranking American to have served on the staff of the United Nations. No one would have guessed, that is, except his grandmother.

"That sounds like my grandma," Joe Joe thought with a grin. Then he read on.

Raised in Los Angeles by his grandmother from the age of thirteen, Ralph Bunche grew up with her belief that education was the key to a good and successful life. Even though he worked at a newspaper after school to help support his family, his grandmother expected him to study hard and do well in school. He did not disappoint her. Ralph Bunche graduated from high school as valedictorian—first in his class.

"When does he start being a peacemaker?" Joe Joe asked himself impatiently. Then he put the book down and started on his own homework.

The next morning, Joe Joe heard his parents talking downstairs in the kitchen as he got dressed and ready for school.

"Joe Joe in trouble," Brandon declared from his seat at the table as Joe Joe sat down next to him.

"No, he's not, Brandon!" his father gently, but quickly, corrected him. Then Dad looked at Joe Joe. "But, there *is* trouble at your school. The letter we got yesterday says that some of the high school gangs are recruiting members. They're worried about fights between rival gangs." Joe Joe's father put down his fork and looked across the table at him. Then he picked up the letter and held it as he looked at Joe Joe.

"Son, do you know what gang colors are?"

"Well, I know KC's gang wears navy blue sweatshirts and caps," Joe Joe admitted. "But I don't know about the rest."

"This letter says that anyone wearing gang colors to school will be sent home. This is serious, Joe Joe. You be careful and don't get mixed up in any of this. Gangs are nothing but trouble. You do the right thing and stay clear of them."

"Yes, sir," Joe Joe nodded, looking his father straight in the eyes. "I will."

"Gang trouble," his mother muttered as she fed Brandon. "School's not what it used to be." Then she said to Joe Joe, "Listen to your father—be careful!"

That day on the way home from school, Joe Joe tried again to avoid Tyrone, but his friend caught up with him.

"I saw some of KC's boys talking to you today." Tyrone paused to see if Joe Joe had anything to say. Joe Joe kept quiet. He just looked down at the sidewalk as they walked along.

Tyrone continued with a frown, "There's gonna be trouble soon, Joe Joe. And I'm gonna be ready. Why don't you come on and be part of my crew? I'm calling us 'The Defenders.'"

"I don't know, Tyrone...."

"What are you afraid of?"

"I'm not afraid of anything!" Joe Joe answered defensively.

"Oh yeah you are," Tyrone taunted him. "You're just scared—a punk!"

Joe Joe stopped walking, his fingers curling into tight fists. No one had ever called him a name like that before.

Tyrone kept on going. "Maybe I don't want you in my crew after all," he declared as he headed for home. "You punk."

Joe Joe just stood there for a long moment after Tyrone swaggered away. He wasn't afraid—not really. But he *was* angry and confused. Tyrone was supposed to be his friend, but nowadays Joe Joe wasn't so sure. He didn't even want to go home yet just in case Tyrone started looking for him again.

The library was just ahead. Joe Joe walked up the steps and sat outside on the stoop. He didn't even want to go inside and talk to his friend Mrs. Morgan. He just wanted to be by himself for a while. He pulled his library book out of his school bag.

Ralph Bunche believed that any success he had in his education and in his life's work was because of the lessons his grandmother taught him and because of the encouragement she gave him as he was growing up. It was his grandmother who had encouraged him to go to college. He did not want to go, but to please his grandmother, he enrolled. To his surprise, he found that he enjoyed college. And even though he continued to work many different jobs while attending classes, once again, he graduated as valedictorian.

It was while in college that Ralph Bunche developed an interest in political science—the study of government and politics. Because he did so well in college, when he graduated in 1927 he was given a scholarship to study political science and international relations at the graduate school at Harvard College. In just one year, he completed his master's degree in political science. These studies prepared him for his future: his life as a peacemaker.

"*Peacemaker.* There's that word again," Joe Joe said aloud. "It's time to go home and talk to *my* grandma," he thought as he picked up his things.

Ralph Bunche in Paris, 1948, as a United Nations mediator, discussing the renewed fighting between the Arabs and Jews.

When Joe Joe got home, his grandmother was standing over the sink, cutting up some cabbage. Joe Joe pointed to the framed embroidery. "Peacemaker. What does it mean, Grandma?"

Grandma put down her knife and faced Joe Joe. "It's easy to be part of a group and let them think for you, Joe Joe," she answered slowly. "But a peacemaker stands away from the group. A peacemaker isn't part of the problem. A peacemaker helps people *work out* their problems."

Joe Joe nodded and asked, "OK, what does *blessed* mean?"

"That's an easy one. It means happy!" she answered with a smile.

Joe Joe looked thoughtful. "Thanks, Grandma," he said as he walked slowly upstairs. He still didn't really understand. He took out his library book again. He wanted to know more about this peacemaker.

Ralph Bunche went back to Harvard to work on his doctoral degree. In 1932, he visited Africa. This was when he began to think of peaceful ways for European countries to leave the African countries and let them, once again, govern themselves. After this visit, Ralph Bunche was able to complete his doctoral work, and in 1934 he became the first African American to receive a doctorate in political science.

"Ralph Bunche started thinking about making peace even before anyone asked for his help!" Joe Joe realized, impressed.

At the end of World War II, countries from all over the world wanted to form the United Nations, an organization that would try to find peaceful ways to end problems between countries. Ralph Bunche was asked to help organize the new group. Then, in 1946 he was invited to stay with the United Nations as it worked for peace around the world. It became his life's work.

Joe Joe closed the book. "Lord," he prayed, "show *me* how to be a peacemaker like Ralph Bunche was. Help me do the right thing!"

Ralph Bunche (right)
in front of the
United Nations building
in New York City
in 1964.

The next morning, Joe Joe got dressed, ate breakfast, and left the house quietly. His parents hadn't even come downstairs yet. He was leaving early so that he wouldn't have to see Tyrone on the way to school. Instead, he saw Kalia.

"Joe Joe, wait for me!" she called out as she hurried to catch up. "You don't usually leave for school this early." She looked at him sideways. "You aren't trying to miss seeing Tyrone, are you?"

"No, I wasn't even thinking about Tyrone this morning," he fibbed, trying to sound casual.

"Well," Kalia shrugged, "I heard Tyrone tell his crew that you're a punk—scared of getting into trouble."

"I'm not afraid of anything," Joe Joe defended himself. "And I'm *tired* of Tyrone calling me a punk!" he added, raising his voice a little.

"Well, he says...."

"Joe Joe, Kalia—how's my crew?" Tyrone asked as he came up from behind. Startled, Joe Joe and Kalia jumped, and Tyrone burst out laughing.

Joe Joe didn't laugh. He looked Tyrone straight in the eyes.

"I'll do it," Joe Joe said abruptly.

"What?" Tyrone was shocked.

"I'll join your Defenders."

"Well," Tyrone smirked, "it's not that easy, you know. First you gotta prove you aren't the punk everyone thinks you are!"

Joe Joe swallowed hard. "So, what do I have to do?"

Tyrone gave him a hard look and asked, "You going to work today?"

"Yeah."

"Then steal something. Take something from old Mr. Booth's store. I'll come by your house later—after work. Show it to me and you'll be one of the Defenders."

The three of them walked on to school. They didn't talk any more about what Joe Joe was going to do that afternoon.

Mr. Booth was waiting on a line of customers when Joe Joe arrived at the store after school. Mr. Booth already had the boxes in the aisles. Joe Joe went right to work taking the cans from the boxes and putting them on the shelves.

As he worked, Joe Joe heard the last customer ask for a special kind of mustard. Mr. Booth told her he would have to check in the back. She told him she would run another errand and return in a few minutes.

"Now's my chance," Joe Joe thought. Mr. Booth was in the back. The store was empty. Joe Joe was all alone. He looked around and spotted a can of tuna fish. It was small enough to fit inside his book bag.

But as he grabbed the can, he started thinking about how much Mr. Booth trusted him to leave him alone in the store like that. And Joe Joe knew that if Mr. Booth ever found out he had stolen something, he would be out of a job. Without a job, he wouldn't be able to save money for college.

Proving himself to Tyrone wasn't worth losing his job. And, more important, it wasn't worth losing Mr. Booth's trust.

"I can't do it," Joe Joe decided. "I won't do it. I don't even want to be one of Tyrone's Defenders—I'd rather be a peacemaker." He turned around, put the can back on the shelf, and finished his work.

When Joe Joe got home, he took his library book and went out in the back yard to read while he waited for Tyrone.

In 1948 Ralph Bunche was given the most difficult assignment of his career. The new country of Israel and many of its neighbors were not getting along. Ralph Bunche's job was to get these countries to sit down together and talk peacefully. To do that, his first step was to reach an agreement between Israel and Egypt. He accomplished this difficult task in 1949. For doing what many thought was impossible, he was awarded the Nobel Peace Prize in 1950. He was the first African American to receive this honor.

"It wasn't easy, but he did it!" Joe Joe grinned as he continued to read.

Because of this success, Ralph Bunche was given the position of undersecretary general in the United Nations. He was then sent all over the world as a peacemaker. He succeeded where many others would have failed because he listened to and respected both sides in any conflict. He was also willing to work as hard as he had to— for as long as he had to—until an agreement could be reached. Ralph Bunche is still remembered today as a peacemaker.

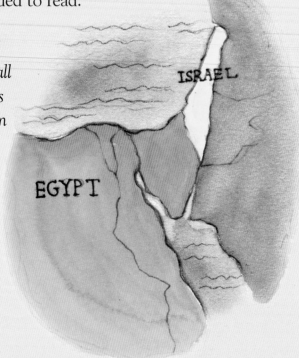

Ralph Bunche (right) was awarded the Nobel Peace Prize in Norway on December 10, 1950.

As Joe Joe closed his book, Tyrone strode into the yard.

"Well, let me see it," Tyrone demanded.

"I don't have it," Joe Joe admitted, standing up and brushing the grass from his pants.

"*What?*"

"I don't want to be a Defender."

"You decided to go over to KC's gang!" Tyrone was furious.

"No, not that either," Joe Joe shook his head.

"Listen, Joe Joe, you can either join me and the Defenders or be a part of KC's gang or the Old Men...."

"Nope—there's another way. I can be a peacemaker," Joe Joe answered.

Tyrone just stared with his mouth open. "*What* is a peacemaker?" he asked finally.

"A peacemaker helps people work things out," Joe Joe explained. "If I don't join up with your crew or KC's gang or the Old Men, maybe other kids at school will see that they don't have to pick sides in the fight or cause trouble either. Maybe they'll see there's another way of doing things."

Tyrone stood there for a minute and then shook his head. "I'd rather be a Defender any day."

"And I'd rather be a peacemaker," Joe Joe responded proudly.

"Man, you're nuts. I'm gettin' out of here." Tyrone turned and walked away.

Joe Joe picked up his book and walked slowly toward the house. Suddenly, he understood the embroidered words in Grandma's kitchen, because he felt good inside. He was happy! *Blessed are the peacemakers.*

He looked up and saw his grandmother standing at the back door. He could tell by the wide smile on her face that she had been listening to him talk to Tyrone.

She opened the door as he came up the steps and said, "Joe Joe, I'm so very proud of you. You're a real peacemaker!"

"I did the right thing, didn't I, Grandma?" Joe Joe demanded, already knowing the answer.

"Yes, Joe Joe, you did the right thing."

He grinned broadly as she reached out, took him in her arms, and gave him a big hug.

MARLBOROUGH PUBLIC LIBRARY
MARLBORO, MASS. 01752